DOES A BEAR POO
IN THE WOODS?

Buster Books

JL — for shy bears everywhere

MB — for Otis And Barnaby —
EVERYBODY needs good neighbours!

Edited by Susannah Bailey

Designed by Jack Clucas

Cover design by John Bigwood

First published in Great Britain in 2021 by Buster Books,
an imprint of Michael O'Mara Books Limited, 9 Lion Yard,
Tremadoc Road, London SW4 7NQ

W www.mombooks.com/buster   f Buster Books   🐦 @BusterBooks   📷 @buster_Books

Text copyright © Jonny Leighton 2021
Illustrations copyright © Mike Byrne 2021

A CIP catalogue record for this book is available from the British Library.

ISBN: 978-1-78055-715-1

1 3 5 7 9 10 8 6 4 2

This book was printed in April 2021 by Leo Paper Products Ltd,
Heshan Astros Printing Limited, Xuantan Temple Industrial Zone,
Gulao Town, Heshan City, Guangdong Province, China.

DOES A BEAR POO IN THE WOODS?

Written by
JONNY LEIGHTON

Illustrated by
MIKE BYRNE

In the deepest of woodland at the start of the day,
When the sun was just rising and making its way,
A shy bear called Barry slept in the trees,
Amongst all the insects, the birds and the bees.

He snored like a lion
with rumbling roars,

Dreaming of honey
all over his paws.

The treetops were Barry's
most favourite place,
He slept with a big sleepy
smile on his face.

But when Barry woke up, he stretched
and he yawned, and growled like growly bears do.

"First job of the day," shy Barry would say ...

But Barry didn't like to poo where everyone could see,
He liked a bit of privacy, how hard could that be?
No sooner had he clambered down, he felt the peering eyes
Of creatures lurking everywhere, the forest full of spies.

So Barry set off through the trees to find a quiet place,
A corner of the woodland, where he could have some space.

Instead he found a flock of birds
who'd do it anywhere,
When woodpeckers weren't woodpecking
they were **POOING** in mid-air.

He tried to find a spot to poo
behind the widest trunks ...

... But was rudely interrupted by some

BOTTOM-BURPING. skunks.

Even in a flowery field he couldn't quite let loose,
Slipping in a **POOEY PILE** left by a giant moose.

Barry threw his head back,
he was desperate for release.

"HELP!" he cried out to the sky,

"I need to POO in PEACE."

Just then Barry spotted the familiar friendly face,
Of wise old Brenda Bigpaw sitting in her usual place.
"Barry, stop your grumbling, there's a place just up the stream,
Where a shy bear can poo happily. It really is a dream!"

So Barry did what Brenda
said and set off at top speed,

Under roots and
over branches ...

... wading through
the tangled reeds.

Finally he came across
the most amazing sight.
"A quiet, lonely cabin!
Good old Brenda, she was right!"

Barry burst in through the door, at last he was alone.
"A private place! It's paradise! My very own

POO THRONE!"

"Ahhh!" he sighed quite happily, as he settled down to rest,
Getting nice and comfortable, "This hideout is the best.
I don't have to go trekking through the forest any more."
At least that's what Barry thought before he heard the cabin door ...

"You'll have to wait," said Barry. "I'm afraid I got here first."
The woodsman sped off quickly with a super-speedy burst.
Barry waved a friendly paw and growled his growly "Bye ...

... I mustn't be the only one around here who is shy!"